ANNE FINE

Notso
Hotso

Illustrated by Tony Ross

PUFFIN

PUFFIN BOOKS

Published by the Penguin Group
Penguin Books Ltd, 80 Strand, London WC2R 0RL, England
Penguin Group (USA) Inc., 375 Hudson Street, New York, New York 10014, USA
Penguin Group (Canada), 90 Eglinton Avenue East, Suite 700, Toronto, Ontario,
Canada M4P 2Y3 (a division of Pearson Penguin Canada Inc.)
Penguin Ireland, 25 St Stephen's Green, Dublin 2,
Ireland (a division of Penguin Books Ltd)
Penguin Group (Australia), 250 Camberwell Road, Camberwell,
Victoria 3124, Australia (a division of Pearson Australia Group Pty Ltd)
Penguin Books India Pvt Ltd, 11 Community Centre, Panchsheel Park,
New Delhi – 110 017, India
Penguin Group (NZ), cnr Airborne and Rosedale Roads, Albany,
Auckland 1310, New Zealand (a division of Pearson New Zealand Ltd)
Penguin Books (South Africa) (Pty) Ltd, 24 Sturdee Avenue, Rosebank,
Johannesburg 2196, South Africa

Penguin Books Ltd, Registered Offices: 80 Strand, London WC2R 0RL, England

www.penguin.com

First published by Hamish Hamilton Ltd 2001
This edition published exclusively for Nestlé breakfast cereals 2006

1

Text copyright © Anne Fine, 2001
Illustrations copyright © Tony Ross, 2001
All rights reserved

The moral right of the author and illustrator has been asserted

Set in Baskerville MT
Printed in England by Clays Ltd, St Ives plc

British Library Cataloguing in Publication Data
A CIP catalogue record for this book is available from the British Library

ISBN-13: 978–0–141–32157–8
ISBN-10: 0–141–32157–1

Contents

1: *How the Horror Began*

SO SUDDENLY ONE morning I'm like, *Scratch-scratch! Scratch-scratch!* and can't stop. It's disgusting.

Everyone else thinks so too.

'Anthony, stop doing that.'

'Would someone please put that pest-ridden dog out?'

'Knock it *off*, Anthony!'

Hey! Notso hotso!

Especially for someone like me. I'm not fussy, exactly. (Personally, I'd call it 'fastidious', though I know one or two have rather harshly used the word 'prissy'.) But I'm not one of those

mucky 'I'm-a-mutt-and-I'll-scratch-if-I-like' pups. I suppose I just think the world's a nicer place for all of us if everyone tries to keep their smells and messes and nasty little personal habits quietly to themselves.

Call me a fuss-budget if you will, but I just like to help to keep things nice.

And skin problems aren't nice. As fellow sufferers will know, skin problems aren't something you can forget for the morning. They drive you mad, especially the itchy ones. First you think, if you just scratch this tiny bit here …

Then you think, if you just have a little go at that itsy-bitsy patch there …

And then you think, now you've started anyway, you might as well scratch sideways on to this bit here …

And before you know where you are, every single bit of you is aflame.

3

I'm not exaggerating. I mean,
AFLAME.

And no one sympathizes. They just
think you're being annoying.

'Anthony, if you don't stop that
dreadful scratching, I'll put you
outside again, even though it's
raining.'

'Anthony! Stop that! Now!'

Talk about a dog's life. If it hadn't been for Moira next door, I might have scratched myself to pieces.

'What's wrong with your dog?'

As if that Joshua would take his eyes off his game for a moment to glance at his own pet. 'Nothing.'

5

'Yes, there is, Joshua. He's dropping weird flakes all over your carpet.'

I'm not even going to *tell* you about the next bit. It's just too horrible. Suffice it to say that it involved an argument about whether or not that stuff all over the rug was actually bits of dead dog skin. And then we had to wait while Moira went home to borrow her granny's magnifier reading glass. And then I had to put up with the two of them endlessly prodding and patting me.

'Ugh! Yuk! That is some sick stuff floating off his back!'

'Gruesome! You ought to tell your mum.'

'Mum? She'd throw up if she saw this!'

Nice, eh? I expect he's forgotten some of his own rather disgusting habits. And as for Moira, well, I've seen her often enough, sitting with her back to the house, doing things to her nose she wouldn't do in front of anyone except me, and possibly Belinda, her pet hamster.

At least the two of them did something useful when my Humiliation Hour was up. They told Her Ladyship.

'Mu-*um*! There's something wrong with Anthony.'

'Yes, Mrs Tanner. Come and look at this. It's *horrible*!'

So Mrs Neglectful finally ambles to the doorway, carelessly dropping cheese from the grater she's holding. (One small bright spot in the day for me.)

'What sort of wrong?'

'His skin's all coming off.'

'Coming off?'

'Yes. In horrible, yukky, revolting little flakes.'

(Well, thank *you*, Joshua. And don't

expect any company or sympathy next time you get chicken-pox.)

'Yes, Mrs Tanner!' chimes in Moira. 'He's all poxy red underneath. And bits of him have gone gooey.'

(Fine, Moira. Just don't sit waiting for me to waste any more of my time fetching sticks to amuse you, next time you're stuck at home with the measles.)

The Kitchen Queen strolls over. I'm hoping she at least has the sense to put the grater down before she touches me. And wash her hands thoroughly after. After all, as I said, I wouldn't call myself *fussy*. But I do like the leftovers that get scraped into my bowl to be reasonably wholesome.

Touching me, nothing! Mrs What?-In-My-House? draws back. 'Ugh! That is *horrible*. That is *repellent*.'

Well, thank you very much. Is there anyone out there, reading this, who's been wanting a crowd of insensitive people?

Because I've got a load here.

A whole *set*.

2: *Getting Worse and Worse*

PERSONALLY, I'D HAVE thought it was an emergency. But not her. Not Lady Laid-Back.

'Is it an emergency?' the vet's assistant asks, down the phone.

'No,' she says. (Just that: 'No.')

And she settles for an afternoon appointment on Thursday.

However, get this. Later that day, when Mr Whoops-Sorry-Forgot-to-Pick-Up-the-Dogfood-Again strolls in from work, she orders him straight back out to buy a pack of hoover bags. 'No, you *can't* leave it till later,' she tells him when he starts grumbling. 'Not with flakes of dog skin all over. This is an *emergency*.'

Not the most sensitive bunch. And don't think I'm making it up when I tell you I haven't been shooed out of the house quite so forcefully or so often since that toddler with the allergies was visiting last Easter.

I made the most of it – even turned

into a bit of a sun demon on the
quiet, after I'd walked past Lady
Vain's fortress of beauty mags on the
landing and seen an article that
claimed that – sensibly handled –
ultraviolet light can work wonders
with what they tactfully call 'iffy' skin.

Though that great snoring slug-
coloured heap on next door's wall did
turn a bit brutal when I stretched out

to offer my poor itching flanks to the
Great Eye of Heaven's healing
powers.

'Looking a bit "bare rug", aren't you, Anthony? Have the family been feeding you Hair-Fall-Out pills?'

'Nice,' I said. 'Coming from a cat that's as big as a barrel.'

'Go gnaw a doorknob, Ant!'

I hate it when she calls me 'Ant'. So I snuck back inside. And got shooed out again. And thought, 'Right, then. It's their fault if I go a-wandering.'

And I went down the park.

I'm not the gang type, on the whole. It's not my scene. I think smell tours are juvenile. When Buster and Hamish and Bella over-excite themselves, their tongues get a bit piggy. And I don't care for the way that, when they're playing *Dingoes v. Jackals*, they leave a trail of mashed bushes behind them.

From time to time, I say a word on the subject.

'Could you take a little more care?' I plead. 'Some of us have to walk in this park every morning. Please try to leave the place as pleasant as you found it.'

They jeer, of course.

'Well, if it isn't Oily Anthony, the Park-keeper's Pal.'

'I'm really, really worried!'

'Oh, bite me! Bite me!'

Most days, our Buster's in his I'm-the-Leader-of-the-Pack mood. I pad up. He turns, gives me the ultra-unfriendly Lost, are you? stare, and says, 'Fell out of your basket, Ant?'

I roll my eyes. I mean, that sort of sarcasm is so ten minutes ago. (Or even earlier.) 'Well, don't you absolutely reek of cool!' I scoff, and

wait for his hackles to rise and that stupid little growl that's supposed to mean, 'Watch it, Mr Nothing from Nowhere-on-Sea,' before he invites me to join them for a bit of a muck-about.

But today, things are different. He's taking an interest, almost.

'What's wrong with you?'

Hamish joins in. 'Yeah. You look weird. Like a bare rug with feet.'

(Just what that nasty cat said. *Now* I'm listening.) 'What do you mean?'

So Bella explains. 'You're missing great patches of fur at the back.'

Hamish agrees. 'You look *terrible*.'

Trust Buster to be a whole lot more unpleasant than he need. 'You told us you were sheepdog-retriever cross,' he crows. 'You never admitted you were one hundred per cent Moulter.'

I'm getting worried now – shimmying round to try and get a look at the bits I've been scratching. 'It can't be that bad, surely.'

'In your dreams!'

'In Never-Ever land!'

'Well, somebody's been putting *something* in your mystery cutlets.'

Up puffs Old Nigel, who's spent the last ten minutes wheezing and staggering over the park towards us at the speed of winter turning to spring.

'My word!' he quavers. He can't take his rheumy eyes off me. 'You look even worse than I feel. I reckon you won't last any longer than I will.'

Talk about *panic*. I just turned and *fled*.

3: *Mirror, Mirror, on the Wall*

SO NOW I'M serious about getting a
proper look at my back and sides. Of
course, since the flaking began, My
Lady Houseproud has kept me right
out of her flouncy-wouncy bedroom
with the floor-to-ceiling mirror. But it's
in there I creep when she's not looking.
(I have to be careful. Last time she
caught me hanging round the door,
she said, 'You so much as *step* in here
while you're shedding that stuff on the
carpets, Anthony, and I will roast you
on a spit!' *And* I believed her.)

So slinky was the word. I made it safely to under the bed. Then out the other side to the mirror.

Oh, horror! Oh, the horror! Imagine sleek and glossy me, twisting my rear end round to take a peek at what was once the perfect hide, and finding ...

Mange!

In places, my bum was raw. If I had been a carpet, you would have tossed me out without a thought. I was appalled. I take my cod liver oil. I get enough fresh air. I exercise. (In fact, of all the dogs round here, I'm probably the most particular about looking after my health and keeping regular habits.)

It wasn't fair. I looked *shocking*. And if I hadn't been exactly where I was most particularly not supposed to be,

I would have raised my head and *howled*.

As it was, I just whimpered.

That's when she walked in. I didn't wait for the rocket I knew was coming. (Something along the lines of, 'Anthony! Didn't I *warn* you that, if you came in here … bleh-bleh-di-bleh —') Tucking my tail between my legs, I slunk

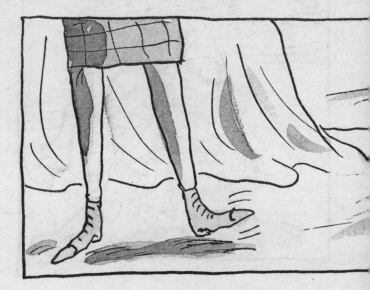

towards the door. Lord knows, I'm no slave to glamour. Ours is a mongrel world, and cross-breeds like myself know only too well that judging by appearances can all too easily lead to –

Hang on a bit! What was this?

Miss Sneak-in-My-Room-and-I'll-Roast-You had thrown herself on to

her knees at my side. She had her arms around my neck, and she was practically in tears herself.

'Oh, Anthony! You poor lamb! You're in *misery*, aren't you? You're actually *whimpering*. Oh, you poor darling.'

And suddenly she's on the phone. 'No!' she's telling the vet's assistant. 'Thursday *won't* do. The poor creature's in agony. I don't care how many people you have waiting. This is an *emergency*, and I'm bringing him *now*.'

Next thing I know, I'm standing trembling on the examination table, and Delia Massingpole B.V.Sc., M.R.C.V.S., is peering at me through a little lens.

'Yes, very nasty. It must itch a lot.'

After five years in vet school? This,
I could tell her for free! But I just
stood there, shedding quietly, while
she looks some more.

Then out it comes. I couldn't bring

myself to listen to the details, so, to this day, I'm not quite sure whether she said it was scabies masquerading as mange with a little touch of eczema, or mangy eczema with a faint veneer of scabies, or all three at once. All I know is, I tried to keep my head high and ponder inner beauty.

Suddenly Ms Massingpole's handing over a giant tub of gloopy-looking yellow cream. 'This should do the trick.'

Lady Lavender-Room-Haze unscrews the lid and sniffs. 'It doesn't smell very nice.'

Hell-*oo*! I'm thinking. The stuff's not supposed to go in your bath. Or on your face. It's supposed to go on my bottom. And just so long as it does the trick, like Vet Massingpole thinks, things are peachy by me.

Miss Shed-on-My-Rugs-and-I'll-Kill-You is still looking dubious. 'How am I supposed to rub it on him?'

I'll sit still, I am promising silently. I will sit *still*.

But that's not what she's worrying about. 'This stuff's so tacky, I'll never get it out from under my fingernails.'

Oh, deary me! I hope you know I'm practically falling off the table here, from sheer anxiety and grief on her behalf. Good heavens! Maybe she'd better take me home straight away, and let me scratch myself *bald*, rather than risk getting even a dab of icky, nasty-smelling yellow stuff under one of her perfect Sugar Frost talons.

'I've got an idea,' said First-in-Command Massingpole. 'We'll shave him.'

Well, whose side's *she* on?

I stare.

And so does Mrs T. 'Shave him?'

'Yes. It's a much better idea.' (I'm frozen with horror. She's plugging in the razor.) 'We'll shave the fur that's

left. That way, the cream will rub in better. The problem will go away faster. And all his fur will grow back soon enough.'

Oh, sure! A primrose plan!

For *her*.

I turn my head to the lady who first

picked me out from behind bars; who
first decided I would be an asset to
her family; who bought me my first
ever real dog bed and my bright red
plastic bowl; who came down *fifteen
times* on my first night, to comfort and
reassure me.

She loves me. I *know* it.

But guess what the weaselly traitress said to Butcher Massingpole?

'Brilliant. Let's do it!'

4: *Talk About* Tough

THEY WERE PITILESS, those ladies. I don't think I've ever put up such a struggle, and I can't remember ever losing a fight so fast.

Talk about *tough*. Milady Massingpole wielded the shaver like someone in a horror film you're too young to watch, and, get this, threatened me with *anaesthesia*, if I kept wriggling!

And the Hand-Cream Queen pinned me down with her elbows. (I take as much care of my paws as the next pup, but really, these perfect fingernail worries of hers are truly getting out of hand.)

Brrrr.

Brrrr.

Brrrrrrrrrr.

BRRRRRRRRR.

I certainly hope nobody ever does anything halfway as brutal to you. When they'd finished, the floor looked like a hairdresser's, the day girls with shiny skulls come back into fashion.

And I was *naked*. My skin looked like plucked chicken.

They broke off for a teensy-weensy discussion about where to stop.

'Are you going to shave all the way down his tail?'

'Yes, I'll just leave the tufty bit at the very end.'

'What about his head?'

Cruella Massingpole inspects my head for more of whatever it is that

38

has landed me in her den of shame.
'He's clear from the neck up. So let's
leave the head, and see how he goes.'

See how he *goes*? Perhaps she means,
see over which cliff he throws himself.
Or see how, with all the stuffing
knocked out of him, he takes to his
dog bed and pines to death quietly.

See how he goes, indeed! He goes
exactly how you'd expect him to go.

Dead fast!

I wasn't going to let those nosy parkers in the waiting room get an eyeful of this spring's new fake-o-la oven-ready retriever look. No, sirree! The minute she'd finished rubbing that disgusting yellow gloop all over my poor shaven body and lifted me down from the table, I shot off.

Taking the Maniac Massingpole

utterly by surprise, I spun round and
dashed between her legs, and out the
back way, past all her shelves of
fancy He-Won't-Even-Notice-This-
Needle-Going-in-Him syringes
(Dream on! We're not all half-dead
like Old Nigel), past lines of cages
stuffed with scowling cats busy
licking their stitches, and out the
back door to the car park.

And there I waited, lurking behind
a large PATRONS ONLY sign, in case
anyone saw me.

Finally, out she comes, all smiles and
wheedling. 'Anthony! Anthoneeee!'

She thinks I'm *stupid*?

I give her a growl. Unlock the car!
it means. Open the door! Let me in,
out of sight, *quick*!

'Oh, *there* you are, poppet!' She's
smiling at me. Mrs Betrayal has the

nerve to *smile*. 'It's all right, darling.
You're safe now. That nasty vet lady
has finished upsetting you.'

I see. She thinks my memory's been
shaved off too. Well, I don't think so! I

seem to remember *two* people bending over me, pinning me down.

Working as a *team*.

(And don't think this doozie'll be hurrying back for his boosters.)

All the way home, I'm planning my next sharp move. If she thinks I'm

going to pad up the garden path with my head held high, she has another think coming. For one thing, the gossip will get round this cul-de-sac like news in a rabbit warren ...

I can see it now. Straight from the headlines of *The Bun*:

Huge, plucked, four-legged chicken sighted in Juniper Close.

In this issue:

Are We in Danger?
And Our Science Man asks:
Has G.M. Meddling Gone Too Far?
See pages 2, 3, 4, 14 & 16.

plus!

Favourite chicken-leg recipes!
Snatched photos in our
special pull-out supplement.
Completely FREE!

No, thanks. I'll nip up the side of the house under cover of the lilacs, hide in the rucksack under the bed in the spare room, and wait till I grow out.

I'm ready. Like a highly trained member of some crack army team, I have my head down but I'm poised to fly. She flaps about a bit as usual, shovelling lipsticks back in her *Parfumerie* under the dashboard, and picking bits of used tissue off the floor.

And then she gets out, slams her door, and comes round the back to open mine.

I didn't mean to shove her into the lobelias. That really wasn't part of the plan. It's just that, as we professionals so often say:

HE WHO DARES, WINS.

And only a greyhound could have come after me. I shot down that side entrance so fast, my slipstream very nearly set fire to the dustbin. I had my eye on cornering at Formula One speeds, jamming myself out of sight between the shed and the wall, and then, when she opened the back door and

started with her pathetic greasy
wheedling –

'Anthony! Oh, Anthoneeeee!'

– hurling myself past her so fast
I'd look blurry.

Who's there to ruin the Great
Plan? What's the first thing I see as
I come out of the straight?

Why, next-door's cat, of course,

idling its life away as usual in one of the sunspots on our wall.

That's *it*, I'm thinking. *Doomed*. The whisper will get down the street so fast that even before Miss I'll-Just-Put-the-Kettle-on-Before-I-Call-Anthony bothers to stroll to the back door, that cat'll be selling tickets:

Come and Laugh at Ant!
Price: Top of the milk
(or a bit of cooked liver).

And what happens?

The weirdest thing. (Maybe a miracle.)

The cat doesn't recognize me.

Does it slap on its usual snooty, Oh-Yawn, It's-That-Wuss-Anthony-Again look?

No, it doesn't. It looks as if
someone has shoved a billion volts of
electricity up its tail.

Does it arch its back and spit
nastily?

No.

Does it hang about sneering?

No, it does not.

It vanishes.

Just like that!

Always good to see the back of
that cat, but, really, this was
spectacular.

It made up for a lot.

As soon as Her Ladyship had stopped
calling 'Anthoneee!', I slunk to the
door. (I wasn't going to have her

think I was obeying orders after the GBH she'd done to me.)

I had a listen. Excellent! She'd gone upstairs to give Joshua some grief for leaving a trail of crisps along the hall and up the stairs. I hoovered my way up after them, and passed his bedroom door while she was still spooning out her motherly lecture.

'… bleh-bleh-bleh-told you once, must have told you a million times … bleh-bleh-bleh –'

Good thing I'd nearly reached the spare room. Already my eyes were glazing over, and boredom was making my legs weak.

But suddenly even the Nagger Queen lost interest in what she was saying. She broke off. 'Oh, never mind,' she told him. 'Come down

and have some tea, and I'll tell you all about this afternoon.'

Explain what a hoot it was, I expect she meant. Give you a good laugh. But there was no time to stand about being bitter. She was already backing out, and there was nowhere to vanish except through the door to her own room.

Abracadabra! I'm gone.

If I was quiet before, now I'm on serious tippy-toes. I know as well as you that anyone who has Yours Truly for a pet can cry 'No worries!' when they spot a bit of finger food at rest on the carpet. So if she was spooning out a ticking off to Joshua for the lightest of prawn-flavoured

crisp falls, I wouldn't want to be the
fellow standing with his head hung
low at the moment she clocks yellow
gloop on her nice scalloped curtains.

No, I gave the soft furnishings the

58

widest berth. I stayed on tippy-toes.
I didn't wag. (No problem there.)

I just prudently removed myself to
the other side of the bed.

Beside the mirror.

Aaaargh!

Talk about fright! I nearly died! I
don't think I've ever felt my poor
heart pound so fast.

Put it this way. You'd guessed
already that the vet had ruined your
looks, and your social life, and any
chance you had of making friends
outside of Ugly Club.

But now you realize next-door's
cat didn't hurry off because you had
problem breath.

Oh, no.

She obviously legged it because
she saw what I was looking at in Ms
Vanity's mirror.

And, four-square in the bedroom,
that's a huge lion.

5: Cat Test

I'M GOING TO speak up for young
Moira now. That girl was *sweet*. After
she'd finished screaming, and all had
been explained, she settled down on
the patio with Joshua, and started to
stroke me.

Actually stroke me.

Not the sticky bits, obviously. (Unless
she had mange too, that would have
been silly.) Just my head and my ruff.
But it was soothing. It was comforting.
It made me feel less like a freak.

And it was Moira who put the idea
in my head.

'Hey, Joshua,' she said. 'Let's take Anthony for a walk down the shops and pretend he's a real lion.'

Down the shops, nothing! I hate down the shops. Over-confident toddlers poking their fingers in your eye. And children the same age as you crooning, 'Oooh! What's his name? Can I stroke him? Will he bite me?' Or that old make-you-growler, 'Is he a boy or a girl?' (Do I *look* like a girl? Oh, yes, maybe. To someone with their head in a bucket!)

Even the get-aways are spoiled, with every shopkeeper making the same old tired joke. 'You should get your Anthony to carry this lot home for you, Mrs Tanner.'

No. I hate down the shops.

But that 'pretend he's a lion' bit – that made my ears prick up. First,

shake off the minders. I acted casual
– you know the sort of thing: 'I'll just
step out for a moment. Call of

nature, you understand. Back in a minute.' They didn't suspect a thing.

Neither did she. Miss Wasted-Enough-Time-on-You-Already-Today opened the back door with barely a word. (How fast sympathy shrivels.)

And I was out.

Cat test!

I must have done a pretty good job first time around, because the charmer wasn't back on our wall as usual, acting the fur slug. The secret of tracking, of course, is: Know Your Enemy. So I thought back to last time Old Tub o' Lard was in a major snit, and that was after it had come back from one of Stitcher Massingpole's cages.

It spent that whole week in the garden shed, licking its wound.

I take a peek. Yes! Door a fraction

open. Tell Sherlock Holmes he needn't come. Anthony's on the case now.

Squeeze through the fence. (That scraped a bit of gloop off both the sides. Time to start watching my weight again!)

Then, *creepy-creep-creep. Creepy-creep-creep.*

(I'm loving this. As you have probably guessed, nobody calls me 'Scary Anthony'. They don't tremble when they see me. And once, when I overheard Bella saying, 'Frightened of his own water bowl!', I noticed that everyone was looking in my direction.)

I'm ready now. What noise do lions

make? I know they roar. But how does that go, exactly? In this house, we don't get to watch much wildlife stuff. She's into cookery and decorating

programmes. He has the snooker on until all hours. And Joshua prefers those cheap and tasteless American comedies.

I think the last time I saw a lion on television was Christmas Eve.

Yes. In *The Lion King*! ROOOOAAAAAAAR!!!!!!!!!!

Not bad, for a first shot. And what with my appearing in the doorway suddenly, good enough for that cat. Another trillion volts! The thing shot up like something in a horror film. (We *all* watch those.) Practically hit its head on one of the unsanded two by four rafters.

Big shock, big noise. Right now, the thing was yowling fit to burst, trapped in its hidey-hole. (Not quite so cosy *now*.)

But I knew, if it caught sight of me

again, terror might fuel enough of its little brain cells for it to catch on.

Hey! Notso hotso!

So, yes. Good practice. *Excellent* rehearsal.

But time to go now.

Time for the Big Show.

6: Fun-Time

I FOUND THEM smelling dustbins.
Honestly! Would you – *could* you –
imagine being bored enough to
smell a dustbin? Nipping from under
Miss Forsyth's holly bush across to Mr
Hall's hedge, I made it to the park
gates without being seen. And while
the three of them were chasing a
couple of pudgy squirrels back up
their tree – as if, gang, as if! – I slid
round the corner the other way.

Into the kiddies' playground.

Hey! Not my fault! Moira's mum
says au pairs get bees in their panty-

hose about things like a spider in the
bath. I grant you, seeing a lion staring
out at you from behind the baby
swings probably sucks big time; but
that's no reason to deafen everyone
on your way out with your horrible
screeching.

The gang came running. (No one
likes missing a bit of tea-time fun.)
But I was thinking this treat was far
too good to waste on all of them in
one big go, so I slid away between
the compost and the gardener's
shed, towards the old bowling
pavilion.

And that's where I bumped into
Old Nigel.

Clearly he'd only been let out to
play about a trillion years ago,
because he was still only halfway
across the fifty yards from his own

house. He stopped for one of his little twenty-minute breaks in between steps. And tried lifting his head. And made an effort to focus.

And then he (sort of) saw me.

And (sort of) stopped.

Dead.

I chose my word carefully there. I don't mean 'froze'. There's something

alive about 'froze'. 'Froze' gives the idea of alert and ready.

Nigel was just … stopped.

I stood and waited. But really, it was about as exciting as watching Granny get ready for bed. So in the end I simply thought, 'I'll come back later,' and rushed away, into the Quiet Dell.

I don't usually take the shortcut
through there, because there's a NO
DOGS sign. But, hey! Today I'm a lion.

And, strolling through, I cause a bit of a ripple.

'Bertha? Is that a *lion* I see over there?'

'It can't be, Gladys. It must be a speck on your glasses.'

'I really do believe it is a lion, dear.'

'Well, if you say so. Do you suppose the poor lamb would like a bit of my sandwich?'

I'm standing waiting to hear more – like, the answer is *yes*, if it's ham or Marmite, but *no*, if it's apricot jam – when, suddenly, into the dell stroll Buster and Hamish. I *ask* you, what is the point of having a NO DOGS sign if everyone ignores it?

And dangling from Buster's mouth was The Lost Bone.

All right. I freely admit it. Lots of bones get lost. We have lost bones all

over. (Somewhere.) But this bone was dead special. It was cooked. And meaty. And it dripped with marrow. And it had been lost for months, since the day Buster buried it because he couldn't manage. (He'd been hoovering up after a party with pizzas and kebabs – I tell you, you watch those skewers: they are *dangerous*.) I'll spare you the grisly details. Let's just say that some of those half-eaten puddings left on the floor behind the sofa had waa-*aaay* too much sherry and coffee brandy in them.

So Buster reeled out in the dark night to bury his bone, and could hardly remember a thing in the morning.

For just a moment, I forgot the lion bit.

'Hey!' I said, friendly as a six-month-old spaniel. 'You finally found the old trophy bone!'

Buster's not listening. One look at

me, the bone's on the grass, and Buster is running.

And Hamish isn't far behind.

I pick up The Lost Bone. Excellent! More fun on Monday, when I am the only one who knows where to find it. I dig a little hole behind Gladys. (It turns out her sandwich is falafel and anchovy, and therefore definitely not for me.) And then I sashay off around the corner.

Only to bump into Bella.

Where flee turns out to get spelled f-l-i-r-t.

She sees me and starts sweeping the path with her eyelashes.

And guess what she says. 'Well, hell-*o*, Big Boy! Fancy a stroll round the litter bins?'

My turn to flee! I made it back to the bowling green, where twenty

Frost-Tops playing a big match
scattered.

    'Lion! Lion on the loose! Lion!'

    'Are you *sure*, Gregory?'

'Lion!'

One of them threw a bowling ball. It kind of rolled up gently between my paws. I tried to roll it back. (Talk about *heavy*, I pushed my hardest and the thing got *nowhere*. These grizzled folk must be a whole lot tougher than they look.)

Not wanting to trash the image, I slid away between the bushes – back into the clearing, where Nigel is still sort of standing there, still sort of *stopped*.

'Nigel?' I said. 'Nigel?'

He's staring at me with those sad old sheep's eyes. But nothing more. Not a flicker.

'Come on, Nigel.' I give him the tiniest of nudges. 'Take a step.'

He rocked a bit dangerously, but nothing else happened.

I went back round the front. He was still staring at me, but he wasn't blinking.

Uh-uh! Notso hotso. I always thought, when there was nothing left to hold you up, you probably fell over. But that's arthritis for you, I expect. It is a *scourge*. Nigel often said as much.

He couldn't stay there, could he? No, of course he couldn't.

And I couldn't carry him.

So I used subterfuge. I stood beside him and I howled. Pitifully! I howled like the Lost and the Damned all herded together. I howled to bring people with stones for hearts running with stretchers.

And, as soon as I heard all the footsteps getting closer, I nipped out of sight in the bushes.

So then it's Action Replay with the adults.

'What's up, old boy? What's all this noise about?'

'Thorn in your paw?'

'Lost one of your puppies?' Closer look. Correction. 'Great, great, great grand-puppies?'

Nigel is saying nothing.

So one of the blokes reaches over to stroke him.

Mistake!

Over he keels.

TIM-*BER*!!!

I won't say the real word, in case we have a few soft-hearted souls out there, reading this at bedtime. (I like to keep things 'family'.) Let's just admit Old Nigel was not exactly in peach form. He wasn't quite himself. His own little personal party was over.

A blessing, really. His life had been
a burden to him for quite a while.
Any responsible owner would have
taken him up to Ms It's-Kinder-and-

I-Assure-You-He-Won't-Feel-a-Thing
Massingpole the very first time he …

Hey! No time for morbid chat! The
speciality howling had brought the
park-keepers running. It was time to
go.

Fun over.

There's not much more to tell. The
chaos I caused made it into the paper.
(I could have done without the word
'mangy' appearing quite so often, but,
hey! That's the tiger of fame: you
can't ride it.) Poor Bella – she was
blushing for a while. (We all call her
The Lion Queen.) I made a deal with
Buster: no respect – no bone, and I
doubt if he'll be teasing me so much
or so often.

And we all went to Nigel's funeral.
(Bit of a 'dig and drop' if you want

my opinion. It could have been nicer, but there you go, if you're not there to see it, I guess it doesn't really matter.)

And, next day, Hamish left his squeaky bunny outside our gate, so I'd have something to do till the old hairs grow back again, and I can come out without everyone pointing.

'See him? I read about that dog in the paper. It seems what happened *was* ...'

It's quite a tale, huh?

But, fact is – it's over.